I0575529

Cover Art: Pgaillustrations

1st edition 2025

 Formatted with Vellum

Stalked Through the Night

DEANN SOLEIL

Contents

Blurb

The Chase is an event that comes once a year to Flowerville this small-town that is open to the public. People come from all over to experience what is hidden within.

For one night only, there are no rules and lines may become blurred. A chance to give into one's deepest, darkest desires and needs.

Will he follow the path of the woods or the path of the cornfield maze, as he is chased by the masked woman?

Tropes & Trigger Warnings

Masked Women

Primal Play

Knife Play

Blood Play

Alcohol Consumption

Mention of a Spider

Dubious Consent

Strangers to Lovers

Dual POV

Edging

Open Door Romance

Toy Play (Corn Stalk)

Quick Burn

Instant Attraction

Secret Billionaire MMC

Therapist FMC

Dedication

*For those women who want to be the chaser for the night
and give into their deepest, darkest kinks and desires,
this is for you.*

Spice Checklist

Chapter 8

Chapter 12

To be chased or

be the chaser?

Prologue

With Halloween fast approaching, a simple event lurks in the nearby woods and cornfields. *The Chase.*

This is one of the most significant events that occurs in the town. It is such a big event that sometimes people from nearby communities even show up to participate.

If someone is lucky enough to participate in it, they will walk away having their deepest and darkest fantasies and kinks come alive. Luckily, this event is a judgement-free zone, so it allows individuals to succumb to what their hearts desire most.

The Chase is a night when individuals of all backgrounds come together to be chased in the most untraditional way. Masked people stalk your every movement until they can catch you in their trap.

Submitting to what happens during these few hours can change your life in ways you may have never imagined.

Those in Flowerville should know what the night brings, but if they don't, they are in for a real treat tonight.

Knives, blood, spiders, and so much more...

CHAPTER 1

Brooklyn

I grew up in a small city in North Carolina, where there were a handful of stores, the smell of manure when you walked outside, and plenty of cornfields. I decided to move away to an urban area to receive my college degree in social work, but everything kept pulling me back to my hometown. Most might find it crazy that I enjoy the aromas from the air, but it's always felt like home to me. I truly can't imagine being anywhere else.

By now, I thought I would have children of my own and a family. Unfortunately, love has never worked for me up until this point. So instead, I decided to open a daycare center and pursue a career as a Licensed Clinical Social Worker on the side. This has allowed me to meet new people and help them navigate through problems they may be having in life.

Being in the daycare center business has been both a positive and a negative. There are so many hot single fathers who bring their children to the center, but I know they deserve more than me. I enjoy being able to engage with these fathers and their children, but I doubt they would ever look at me like that. I feel like I don't match their standards of a perfect woman.

I have tried out relationships with guys in my city; however, they never seem to work out. They either don't know how to work their way around a woman's body, or they treat women like trash. Perhaps having an older man can bring me what I need and help me avoid wasting my time on those who are inexperienced.

As a twenty-five-year-old, my friends always tell me that I need to get out of my comfort zone and engage in activities that some people wouldn't dare to do. This would help me meet new people, instead of living in a bubble of what is normal to me.

People who don't know me assume I'm shy because I often keep to myself or stay with the same friend group. Little do they know, I'm always open to fun and trying new experiences with people. I am what is often referred to as an undercover freak.

I can be fun, and with Halloween coming up, I'm ready to let my inner beast come out. Each year, an event known as The Chase occurs within the city. This event allows masked men to hunt women throughout the outskirts of town and do whatever they want to them, but this year, it will be different. Officials are asking women to step up and take the opportunity to give in to their deepest desires and stalk the men through the night. This allows us to be in control and not submit to what a man needs.

People know what they are signing up for by being a part of this event. It is clearly advertised and explained, so nobody can say they weren't told what to expect.

In the past, there have been people who have come out wounded but never harmed in a manner where they would be unable to walk or function. This event is meant to be fun and allow people to explore kinks that some might not be able to experience on a daily basis. There are also some individuals who have been dying to try out new things but haven't had the chance to.

I know I need to participate this year and be in charge. Unfortunately, I haven't been with anyone recently, so I need some type of release that is going to help with the sexual tension I have been experiencing.

I think about what my goal for the event would be and what I would want to impose on others. This event has been going on for nearly five years now, and I have only participated twice, so I have an idea of what typically happens, but things can change. Having women in control can allow the men to be at our mercy and listen to what we want them to do, so I am excited.

I, for one, am into knife and blood play. I know how to make the perfect cuts without causing too much harm to another person. I might have played around a little with my ex-boyfriend, making him scream out my name as I swiped the knife across his skin. The smell of blood that comes out with each cut just does something to my body. Unfortunately, he wouldn't return any of the favors that I wanted, so that relationship didn't last too long.

I know I need to participate in The Chase to let my darkest desires come out and explore things I have not been able to explore in a long time. Maybe this time, I can find someone willing to get down in the ways that I am. Being able to release my inner kinky self is one of my top goals this year.

CHAPTER 2

Brent

I've always been known as the party guy to my friends and family members. There's something about being out on the town that makes me happy and allows me to express myself fully.

My friends and I are always exploring new places but also frequent some of the local joints. I'm big on hitting the bars and drinking different beers because it gives me an escape from the world. The hazy beers are just so good and aren't too hoppy compared to some of the other beers that I have tried.

Alex, Nate, and Michael are some of my closest friends, but Michael and Nate always have to encourage Alex to go out. The only one who puts up a fuss is Alex because he constantly wants to play a round of pool and doesn't want to drink like the rest of us. Don't get me wrong, as much as I enjoy playing pool, I have a bad habit of hitting the eight ball into one of the pockets, so none of the guys ever want to be on my team.

Tonight, while we're out hitting the bars, I give in to Alex's wants and played a round of pool, and surprisingly to both of us, I do better than normal. Throughout the night, I have been chugging down these beers. I'm still able to function, so the guys know that I am still good for now. A few more drinks might be another story, but I know how not to overdo it.

After a while of talking, I bring up The Chase to the guys and explain how the roles have been reversed this year. The guys seem shocked when I tell them about the reversal and discourage me from going. I have only participated once in the past when I chased one of the hottest girls throughout the woods.

I have been going back and forth about whether I want to participate this year, but I know the guys won't do it with me, so I am in a bit of a dilemma. This is one night out of the year when I can be free, so I feel like I should do it, but I'm not 100% sure.

With contemplation still on my mind, we decide that we are going to call it quits for the night, and everyone heads back to their homes. Ultimately, I decided that I don't want to go home. Instead, I head to the site where The Chase is occurring tonight and text the guys that I made it back home, so they don't worry. They'll probably be angry if they find out that I came here.

Is this a good idea for me to be doing after drinking tonight? Probably not, but I am capable of running through the wooded area tonight. I can luckily still function after a night of drinking. I am able to think straight, I am just feeling good from the slight buzz I have.

The guys often get worried about my drinking habits, but I know I will be fine because I don't always overdo it when I am out. Apparently, alcoholism is prevalent within my family, so I watch my intake to ensure I do not become addicted like my uncles are. I will say that sometimes it is necessary to go on a drinking spree for a celebration or a life accomplishment, but I am careful when doing it.

I push those thoughts out of my head and set foot on the path to where the event is taking place tonight.

CHAPTER 3

Brent

When I get to the cornfield where tonight's festivities are being held, I notice there is a decent turnout of both men and women. I feel like this year, there are more participants than there were the year I came. Maybe it is because the women are in charge this year, so people are interested in seeing how it differs from the past. Having this switch up may also bring more people because they can switch the dominant and submissive roles that typically are seen and experienced during this event.

The women are all lined up with their masks on to ensure that nobody can see their faces. I will never understand this because depending on a person's mannerisms, you can still tell who they are. I guess they want to keep the identities of the chasers hidden, even though you know who the people being chased are. It just doesn't make sense to me.

While waiting for the announcer to talk about the event, I notice three women wearing similar outfits next to each other. One of them stands out to me more than the others. This woman is standing in the middle of her friends with a tight, short, red romper that shows her cleavage, with a black and red mask covering her face in its entirety. The tattoos that line her arms make her look like the most baddest woman out here. I know right then and there that I want her to chase me.

There is something about tattoos that instantly draws me to someone. I have neck tattoos, but to see a woman with a full sleeve makes me want to memorize and kiss each one of them. I don't know what it is about them, but they just make me feel some type of way and can open up hours of conversations.

My mind starts to wander, but I quickly bring myself back to the here and now. There is just something about her that is sending chills through my body and making my dick harden in my pants. That probably shouldn't be happening since she hasn't even touched me yet, but the way her romper is hugging her curves is turning me on more than ever right now. I can't wait to see where the night goes and who she ends up picking tonight.

I genuinely hope it's me. I will consent to any and everything she wants to do to me because, at the end of the day, that is why we are here.

The Chase is something that brings people out of their shells and allows them to do something they wouldn't do on a regular basis. Although my friends aren't here to experience this moment with me, I know I will have fun. I wish they would have approved my want to participate so I can share the stories of what happens tonight with them.

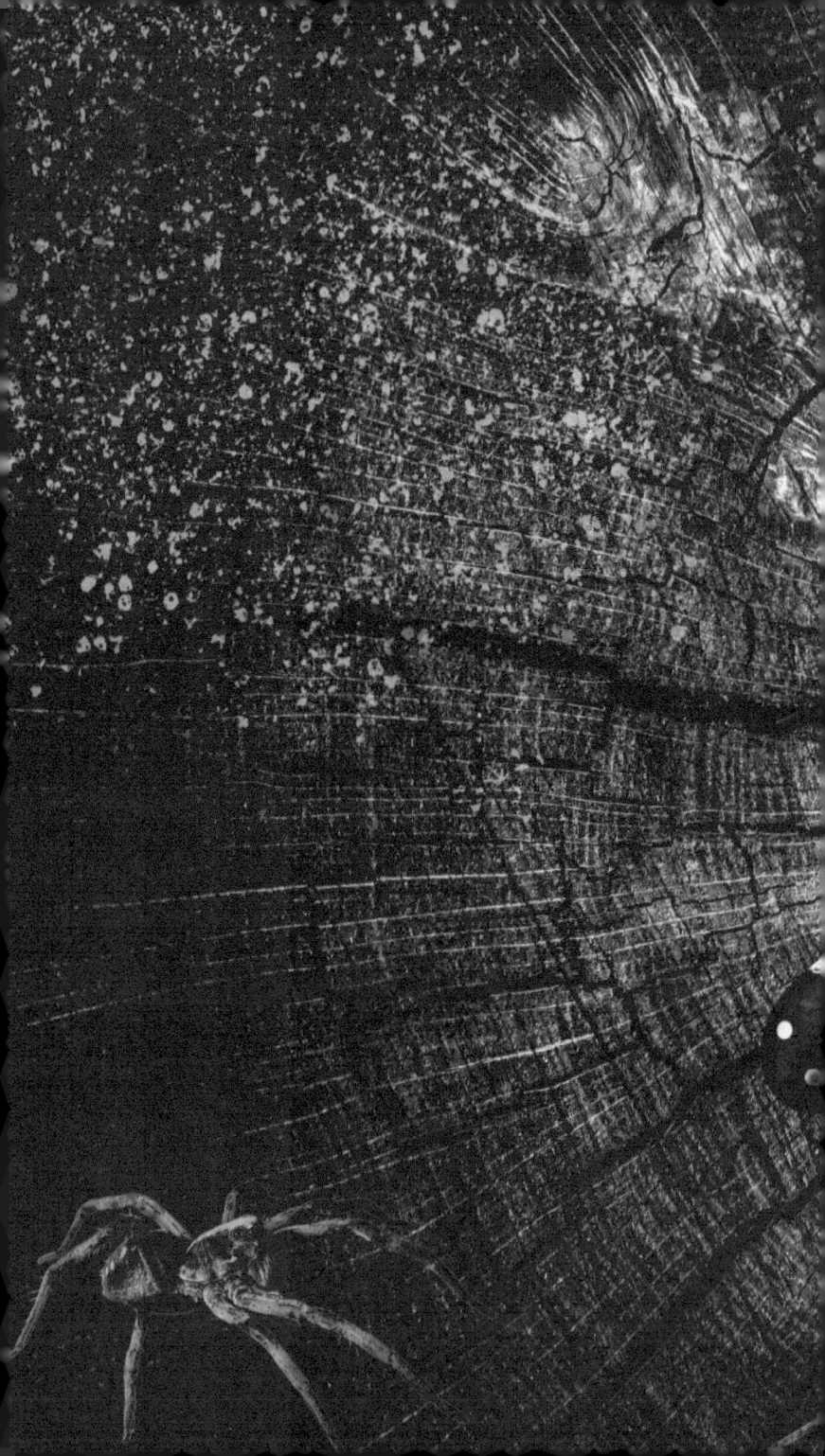

CHAPTER 4
Brooklyn

After talking with my friends, the three of us decided to participate in The Chase tonight. We all think it will be a good idea to let loose after a busy day of work. What better way to do this than being out in the cornfield maze hidden in the woods, having fun.

Being a native of this area gives me somewhat of an advantage because when I was younger, I would come out here every fall and go into the maze. I pretty much know where all the right turns are, but of course, I'm not going to tell others that. I don't know why they haven't changed up the routes after all of these years, but hey I'm not complaining since I have an advantage.

My friends and I each have some distinctive characteristics, such as the two sleeves of tattoos on both of our arms and others along our bodies. I am sure that nobody is going to pay much attention to detail though. Instead, they are going to be more focused on the game of cat and mouse and trying to escape. I like to stay hidden most of the time, so if someone knows who I am, then I will be shocked.

I decided to wear a short red romper that hugs my curves and shows a decent amount of cleavage and a red and black mask that covers my face completely. I went back and forth about what to do with my hair, ultimately deciding to allow my blonde wavy hair to hang down my shoulders. This is probably a bad idea because I could get hot running, but hopefully I will be fine.

I love all the red because it goes with one of my favorite kinks, blood play. Some might not be into blood, but the way it smells and tastes on my tongue makes my body go crazy for more. Call me weird, but I don't give a fuck. I hope the guy I choose tonight is okay with what I have planned for him because if not, that sucks for him.

After mingling with the other girls here, my friends and I line up for the event with me being in the middle. We all have similar outfits on, but in different shades with masks that match our outfit colors. We like to match as much as we can when we go out to events, because we are often categorized as

The Alpha Triplets. We are always known to come together and dominate anything that we're faced to do, so the name is definitely fitting.

This time last year was an experience. I learned how to overcome my fears of spiders during the event. The man who was chasing me had a tarantula with him that he let roam my body when he caught me in the cornfield maze. Who the hell would have thought to bring a spider with them to an event?

I had never been one for spiders before because they always freaked me out, but the way its legs caressed my skin made me feel better than any other object or creature that had touched my body before. It was just different, but different in a good way. If I could experience that pleasure again, then I definitely would.

I do enjoy being in this setting where everyone is focused on doing their own thing, such as the spider experience in the past. I am always on the lookout for information on when the event comes to Flowerville, because I know it will be an experience of a lifetime.

My friend Kelly told me about a time when a guy used a cornstalk to get her off. When we had that conversation, I knew I needed to experience that myself. If I get lucky and have time, that is something that I plan on incorporating into tonight with whoever I match up with.

Tonight is about having fun and not thinking about what happened yesterday, earlier in the day, or what is going to happen tomorrow. I want to just have fun making a guy feel good and allowing them to do the same with my body. As long as I can set the rules, I am fine.

Maybe I can make this an every-year tradition moving forward if they keep it this way.

There are some people who come out who are experienced, while for others it is their first time. The man who I have my eyes set on for tonight seems so nonchalant like he doesn't care about what is going to happen tonight. He is probably a regular here. Little does he know, I have big plans for the two of us.

I know the cornfield maze like the back of my hand, so there is no way that he will be able to escape me. The way he is standing there with his blue shirt, black pants, and tattoos on his neck has me wanting to run over to him now and get the night started. If I could have him every year, I would.

I feel like I might have seen him before, but honestly, each year becomes a blur after a while. My body is often on a high that I can't explain when I finish with the festivities. Tonight will be different, though, because he is mine and I set the pace.

I'm so ready to see where this night goes from here on, and if he easily gives in to my touch.

CHAPTER 5

Brent

I stand here thinking about what the night might bring for me.

I have this premonition that I definitely made the right choice by coming and wild stuff will go down. I don't regret my decision to be here at this moment. Maybe tomorrow, when everything is said and done, I will meet with them and tell them about tonight.

I can tell that the night is about to begin when I see the women in various outfits and masks line up in front of us. The woman who caught my eye earlier seems to be looking right in my direction. It is hard to tell though because I can't see through the eye holes of her mask. If she is staring at me under the mask, then that only makes this decision feel so right.

Maybe she is feeling the same way I am right now about wanting to be matched up for the event tonight. She seems like she knows what she is doing, almost as if she has been here and done this before. I guess one can say experience comes in handy sometimes..

The announcer of the event comes over the loudspeaker, bringing everyone's attention to him. He explains what the night consists of and how the ladies are in control this year.

"If you have been to The Chase in previous years, you know there are usually masked men involved, but this year, we decided to change things up to let the males participate and experience some of their kinks. Men, you will have a two minute head start to allow you to run through either the woods or the cornfield maze, but if you get caught, then ladies, they are all yours. The path you choose is completely up to you. Remember, by participating, you consent to whatever happens while you are engaging in the event. If you decide you no longer want to partici-pate, you have that option as well. I hope you are all ready because your time starts now," the announcer finishes with the sound of an air horn.

A few of the men don't move, as if they are stunned by what the announcer just said.

Now means let's go in my mind, so I don't know

what is causing them to freeze in their places like they have seen a ghost. This year is going to be fun because we have the choice of what route we want to take, instead of being told where to go. This is something that never happens.

I opt for the maze because it adds a challenge, not knowing which route is wrong versus which one is right. Maybe I can convince her to go against the rules and let me bring her pleasure, but I won't get my hopes up too high since tonight is her night. I've always been the type of guy who wants to do more giving than receiving, so I want to be able to do that tonight if she will let me.

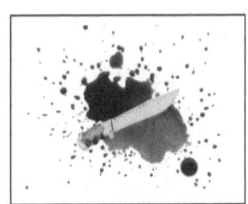

When I begin my trek towards the cornfield maze, I look behind me to the start area and see the woman still facing me. I wonder if the ladies were able to get the same practice that us men used to before the festivities. This allowed us to practice running through the areas where the events took place so we could familiarize ourselves with the routes. If they had this opportunity, then she would have the advantage tonight since I can't remember every twist and turn.

Even if that is true, I can't let those thoughts get the best of me.

As I start to enter the maze, another air horn sounds, which means the ladies have been able to begin their run. I feel like we didn't get too much of a head start, but I guess it is fine. I'll find a way to lose her and hide in different areas of the maze where she might not be able to find me.

Since this maze is in the same setting as the past years, I have some knowledge on where to go. I feel like most mazes are similar because you have to go one way or the other to get out. Once I escape, then I don't have to worry about what could be done to me. But maybe, just maybe, I don't want to escape.

I am so used to pleasuring other women during events like this, but I truly think it would be fun if I could get the same or better experience than in past years.

I don't want her to be afraid to use my body in the ways that she wants to. If she has something that she wants to try out, then I want her to do those things to me.

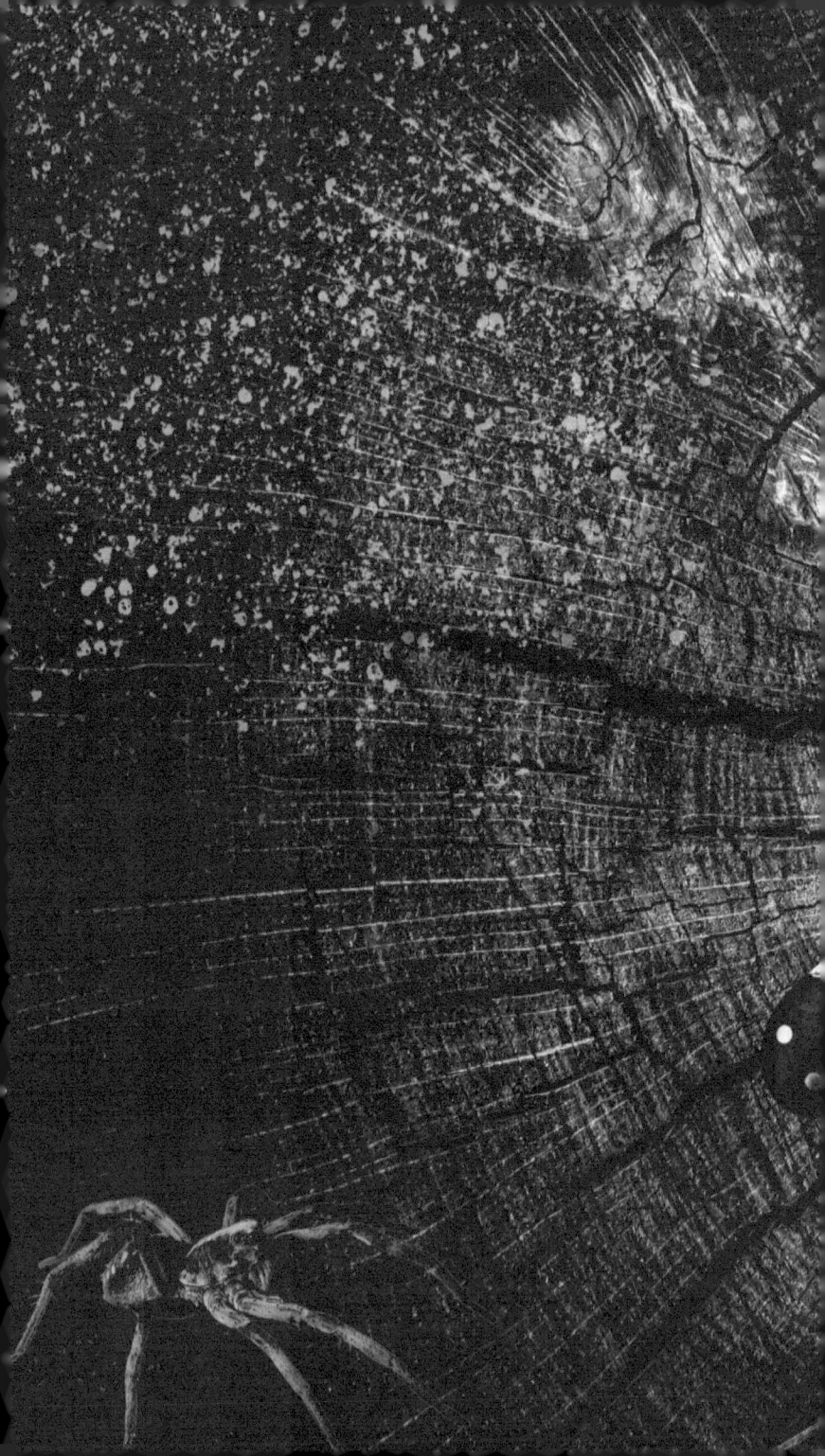

CHAPTER 6

Brooklyn

I n this event, we talk about who we plan on going after, but the men don't know who we pick until they see us going after them. I keep making eye contact with this man to show that I want him, but I keep forgetting he can't see my eyes through my mask. I can tell he sees me focused on him though. Luckily, there isn't anyone out here who is in objection to my choice, so it works out perfectly for me.

When the air horn sounds, and the man before me starts his run, there is something familiar about him and the way he moves. I can see his tattoos at a different angle with each step, and realize that it's Brent.

I've heard so many good things about him in the past during these events and how good he is to the women he interacts with. Someone said that he's a gentleman and when a girl wants something, he will give it to her. That is something that I need in my life.

Shit, just the thought of that has me wishing the roles were reversed and he could spend time in between my legs while caressing my body, but I know that isn't the case.

On second thought, I am in control tonight, so if I want him to devour me, then he will.

I know I will be implementing new things in some way or another tonight. It is so weird because I haven't experienced everything I want to try tonight, but the videos that I have watched have gotten me so wet that I know I need to try it out myself.

My mind continues to drift away to the possibilities of what could happen tonight until Kelly brings me back into focus. "Come on, girl, get your head in the game. He is going to get away if you don't pick it up," she warned. I know I should listen to her because she always has better insight than me when it comes to stuff like this, but those distractions are making me picture how the night can be.

I snap myself back into what is going on in front of me. I focus on Brent's movements and see he is headed for the maze instead of going through the open woods like most of the other men did.

If only he had known before how I had this maze memorized, he might have picked a different route to take. I begin to slow my pace when I get to the entrance of the maze because I want to see if he can get a little bit ahead before I ruin him for the night.

He probably won't get too far, but it is worth the try. When I catch him, he is going to regret taking that path.

Not all girls who look innocent on the outside are innocent on the inside. If people in this town knew the plans that I have tonight, then they would probably lose their minds and be filled with confusion, but fuck what other people think. At the end of the day, a girl has to find pleasure somewhere, and tonight, that pleasure is going to be with Brent.

Allowing him to think he's ahead of me adds to the thrill of what is going to happen for the both of us tonight.

CHAPTER 7

Brent

As I am navigating through the maze, I ask myself why I took the most confusing route. I could have taken the easy way and just run through the woods. But no, I wasn't thinking that way at the moment. The complexities and the thrill are what get me going.

I look around me and see that there is no one else who has decided to take the path that I did. That can be both a good and a bad thing. I like the idea of having this space all to ourselves, but I also dread that others can't hear my screams if they come up.

What do I look like screaming anyway? I think to myself.

This isn't my first time being in this situation, but it is my first time being on this end of The Chase.

I hear a low-pitched voice taunting my name. "Brent, I know you are in there." How the fuck does she know my name? I know I didn't say it out loud. She must have seen me around somewhere in town. That will be a conversation I am going to have to have with her when I finally come face to face with her.

I pick up my speed when I am faced with a cross-road where I don't know which way to go. I know mazes always have dead ends, so I have to pick the correct route, or this could really go downhill quickly.

I go right and hope that is the way to go. I start to make a few strides and find out that this is definitely not the way I should be going. When I turn around, I instantly feel a small hand on my body as I come face to face with a black and red mask.

I wish I could see what is under her mask because the view of her curves is making me want to give in to whatever she has coming for me, but I know I can't right now.

Everyone who knows about The Chase knows that we are subject to whatever those in charge want to do to us. One thing I have found recently is I have both an edging and blood kink. Some people might find those weird, but in this setting, every-thing is fair game. I might be a little crazy, but I want this woman to help me explore my wants and needs.

"Hey, beautiful," I say when I get out of my thoughts. She doesn't say anything immediately, but instead, she pushes me up against one of the corn stalks nearby.

Boy, am I ready for what is to come next? It is a little intimidating seeing her stare into my eyes through the mask without a word, but maybe it won't be too bad in the end.

This might just be her way of preparing me for what is to come.

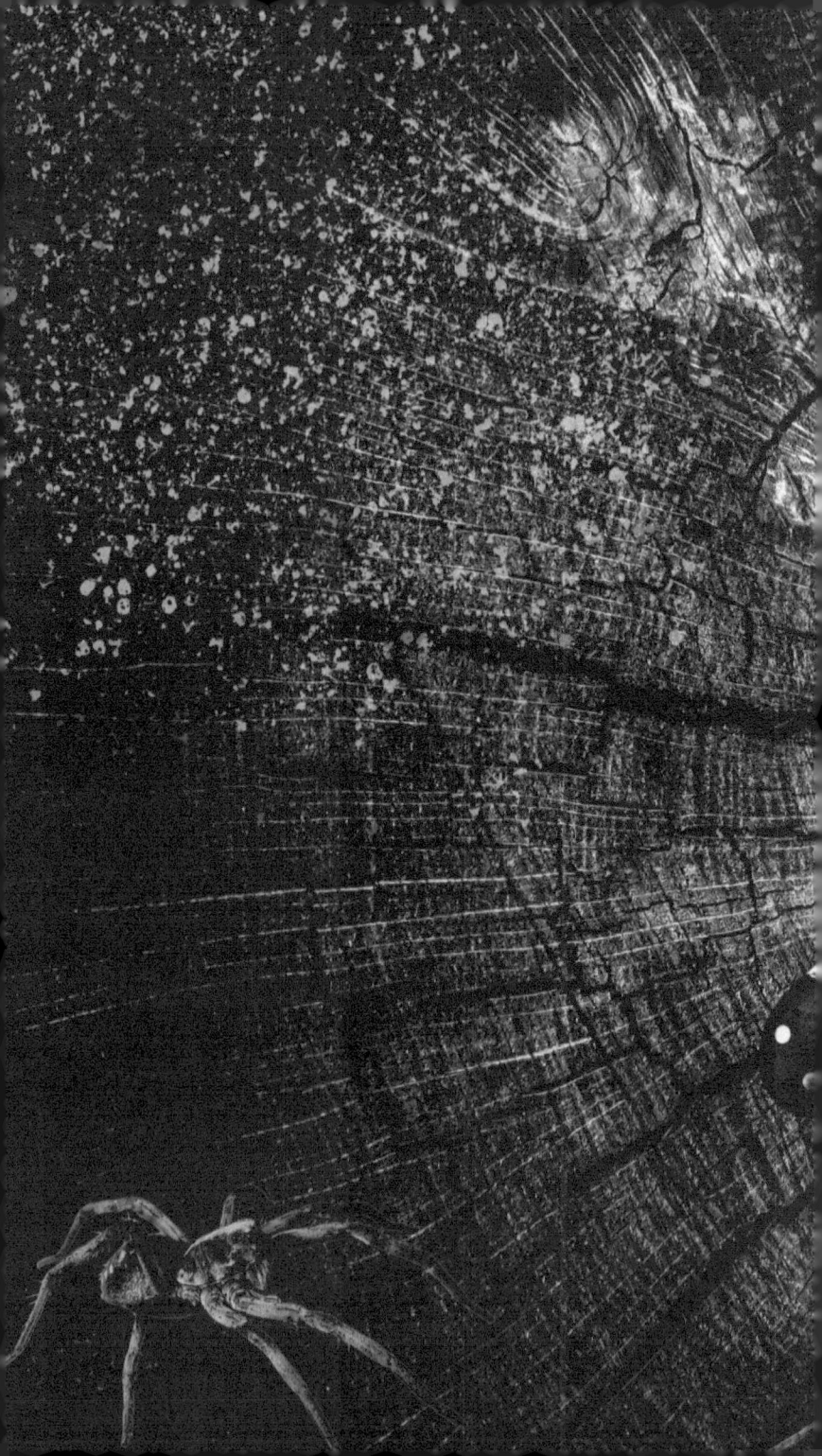

CHAPTER 8
Brooklyn

Him calling me beautiful is doing something to me. He doesn't even know what I look like under this mask, but he is already complementing me. This is something that I wish would happen more.

I often feel insecure about myself, so being here today can take my mind off those negative thoughts I frequently have. There are moments when I feel like nobody will want me because of the way I look, so getting out here can help me push those thoughts to the back of my head. Tonight is about me and being my true self.

I intently stare at Brent, thinking of what I want to say or what I should do first. I am not one to always get right down to business, but there is something about him and his vibe that makes me want to go all in. Maybe I am crazy, or perhaps I am just being me. I have nobody to impress tonight, so why not just do whatever I want to.

When I push him up against the corn stalk, I can see the hunger growing on his face. One thing about being here in The Chase is that consent is given when one agrees to participate unless they decide to stop participating. This allows me to do what I want to and have fun while doing it.

I decide to begin slowly with him to not let him see how dirty I truly can be. I'm tired of being the girl people view as being timid and innocent. Tonight is my night to be the freak I know I can be.

"Take off your shirt," I demand.

He happily obliges.

This is going to be easier than I thought if he listens to me this easily. I don't want to come on too strong, but I think I am ready to speed things up tonight and start to have the fun that I know both of us want to experience.

I grab my knife from the inside of my romper and begin to lift it up to his chest. Outside of my ex, others I have been with weren't down to explore what I want. Tonight, I am definitely about to change that and focus on what I want to do first, then what my partner wants to.

Brent's eyes get wide when he sees the knife

coming close to his skin, but he doesn't do anything to push me away.

I slowly take the knife and make a cut that is less than an inch in length along the side of his chest. The smell of metallic sends tingles through my body, causing my need to taste it to intensify. I take my pointer finger and glide it across the blood, glistening across his chest, and slowly suck my finger.

"Mmmh" is the only word that comes out of my mouth. The taste is delicious, and I can't wait to see what else I can get into with him.

I have never been one to completely comply with what is set for me, so fuck the game. I know what I want tonight, and I won't let some announcer dictate that the women are the only ones in charge tonight. If I ask Brent to get on his knees and take me to the edge, then that's what I'll get.

CHAPTER 9

Brent

The way she just cut the side of my chest and tasted my blood has my dick hardening. I don't think she fully knows what she is doing to me because my jeans are hiding my erection.

There is something about the sight of blood that has me turned on, whether it is my own or someone else's. I feel like since she was able to taste me, I should have the opportunity to do the same for her.

I know she is supposed to be the one who is taking the lead tonight, but I just want to take her right here and right now in this corn maze. I want to make her scream out my name and continuously beg for me to give her every inch of me, but I know I should just sit back and see what happens next.

"Darling, can I ask what your name is?" I choke

out while my brain is still going through a whirlwind of emotions. She begins to hesitate for a brief moment before she says, "Brooklyn." *What a beautiful name.*

The things I would do right now to have Brooklyn amp this experience up would make things so much better for the both of us, but I know patience is needed. There are things I could do that would make this experience so much better for both of us, but I need to be patient because Brooklyn is in charge. We have all night long to give in to what we both want and need.

I go to put my hand on her shoulder but quickly learn that is not the right move when she goes to swat at my hand. *Whoops.*

"Keep your hands off until I tell you that you can touch me," she expresses with a slight attitude in her tone. I didn't mean to make her angry, but I thought a little touch would make her feel more relaxed tonight. I guess not.

I quickly apologize for my actions towards her and stand there waiting to see what she wants to happen next.

CHAPTER 10
Brooklyn

I might have overreacted a little when I swatted at his hand. I just wasn't expecting him to try to touch me, even if it was just my shoulder. I'm here tonight to try different things with someone I may or may not see again, so I need to find a way to loosen up.

Luckily, I have a flask with vodka stashed inside of my romper. I quickly pull it out and down the shot of vodka waiting for me. I let out a sigh as I feel the burn going down my throat. I hope this lets me calm down a little bit and open myself up to the possibilities of what both Brent and I desire. I don't know why I felt so prepared starting off, then all of a sudden I got nervous.

"I'm sorry, I am a little on edge tonight. I'm not used to being in charge, so sometimes, when people touch me, it can be hard for me to have an appropriate response to it. I am so used to men using me however they want to, so that came to the forefront of my mind when you placed your hand on my shoulder. I will be better, though. I want this night to be one that we remember for months to come," I say.

I see him tense up with sad eyes, not knowing what to say to my confession. I don't want to interrupt the moment by making him feel uncomfortable, so I lift my mask to the point where only my mouth is exposed and lean in for a kiss. He instantly places his lips on mine, and we interlock our tongues together in a deep, passionate kiss.

This kiss is something that I have not experienced in a long time, causing me to not want to pull away. I get lost in our kiss, forgetting that we are supposed to be playing a game of chase through this maze. I ultimately end up pulling away and begin to pepper kisses along the tattoos that run down his neck while moving my fingers down his chest.

The definition of his abs has me wanting to lick up the rest of the blood that I created on his chest, but I don't want him to think I am too weird right now. Instead, I lean in close to his ear and whisper, "Run."

CHAPTER 11

Brent

That kiss that we shared made me feel like I was in a different universe. Her lips were so soft that when she pulled away and started to kiss down my neck and chest, it sent chills all over my body. This girl does not know what she is doing to me. Hopefully, she lets me show her soon enough.

As I get lost in the thoughts of what she can do to me next, she tells me to run. At first, I don't budge as I am lost in a trance, but I am soon brought back to reality when she pinches my arm.

I instantly start to move my feet in the other direction of the maze that I should have taken in the first place, so I wouldn't have gotten trapped. I look back and notice that she hasn't started to move yet. I like this because she is giving me a chance to actually get away. That is the best way to be involved in a chase. You want the playing field to be even and give someone some type of chance.

I take different turns through the maze, and before I know it, I am hit by another blockage on the road. *You have got to be kidding me.* I was supposed to get ahead of her, but of course, I would take another turn that I shouldn't.

As I am contemplating what to do, I can hear the screams of other men around me. Whatever they are going through, I can't tell if it is pleasurable or painful. All I know is that I want to experience a little bit of both.

When I turn around, Brooklyn is there, but her mask is covering her face again. Maybe before the end of the night, I will get to see what she looks like under her mask because her name does not sound too familiar to me. Plus I want to see the woman behind this sexy body.

"Take off your pants," she demands. I knew this was going to come, but I didn't think it would happen this fast. Part of me wants to keep my pants on to hide what is growing underneath, but the other part of me knows that if I don't comply, then things could be worse for me. Due to that, I do as she says.

In one quick movement, I remove my jeans, and all you can see is my hard dick poking through my underwear. I wish I could see her facial expression completely because I'm not exactly small. I may be a little cocky at times and some women love it, so I wonder how she will react.

She is definitely in for a treat tonight.

CHAPTER 12

Brooklyn

Oh boy, I'm happy that I told Brent to take off his pants because what I can see through his underwear has my mouth watering for a taste.

I slowly approach him and begin to lower myself to my knees.

When I get down on my knees, I pull his dick from his underwear and gasp in surprise. He is so big. I am afraid that he is going to kill me with how massive he is, but I put those thoughts behind me, lift up my mask a little, and take him into my mouth. I begin to lick the sides of his shaft before I move his hard length in and out of my mouth. I can hear soft moans coming from him.

I continue to take him deeper and deeper into my throat as I begin to cup his balls with one of my hands, causing his body to start to shiver. Who would have thought I would be the one to bring a man to the brink of an orgasm so fast. I can see the frustration on his face as he tries to hold back his moans and his release, but as I pick up my speed, he can't hold back anymore.

He tries to grab my head back to pull away, but I don't let him. I want to see him cum before I let him do anything to my body.

A few seconds go by, and I feel the warm cum shoot into my mouth, causing me to drink him down. He attempts to grip my hair as his body shakes with his release, but I don't let him.

I think I'm going to have a fun time tonight torturing him, but he will definitely have his chance to return the favor when I give him the go ahead.

Once his body begins to return to normal, I can see the hunger in his eyes with the need to touch me.

"Brooklyn, I need you," he says in a stern tone. *I need you too,* I think to myself, but don't say the words out loud. I don't want him to think I am desperate to take him already. Instead, I take my knife back out and make another cut into the other side of his chest.

This one isn't too big, but his blood begins to slowly ooze out of the wound that I made. I have another taste of it, and then I make a small cut into my arm. I rub my finger through the blood from my arm and put my blood-covered finger into his mouth, so he can have a taste as well.

I watch him as he devours my taste into his mouth, licking up every last drop.

CHAPTER 13

Brent

This girl is going to be the death of me. The way she took me down her throat had me feeling like I was in a different universe. Then, when she put her bloody finger in my mouth, it just did something to me. I knew I had a blood kink, but her actions tonight are really showing me how much this kink exists.

Now that I know what her blood tastes like, I want to taste other parts of her body too. I decide to see how far she'll let me go, so I grab her wavy blonde hair with one hand and tilt her head back with the other as I begin to pepper kisses along her neck.

I can tell this is having some type of effect on her, so I don't want to stop. She is in control tonight, but she seems to be submitting to my touch.

I continue to kiss down her neck until I reach her cleavage that is sticking out of her tight romper. I begin to unzip the romper, but she stops me and asks, "Are you sure about this already?" *Fuck, I know I am sure about this.*

I nod my head yes, that I am sure, causing her to allow me to continue to unzip her romper. I shake my head because she leaves nothing to the imagination. She has no bra on, causing her nipple piercings to be on full display for me.

This girl is going to get me in so much trouble. I decide to take her left nipple in between my fingers while I bring the other nipple to my mouth. I suck gently and pull out just enough to blow on it, causing chills to go down her body. "Brent, I want you," she moans out.

This is not the way I saw the night going because I thought she would be in charge and play a little hard to get, but I will comply with whatever she wants me to do to her. She begins to pull away from me as she starts to take off the rest of her romper.

Damn. She has no panties on either. This girl really was prepared tonight to give easy access to all parts of her body.

Brooklyn takes my right hand and allows me to

rub down her body. I slowly inch farther and farther down, stopping just before her pussy.

"Are you sure you want me to take the lead? If I do, I don't know if I will be able to give up control after I stop," I let out.

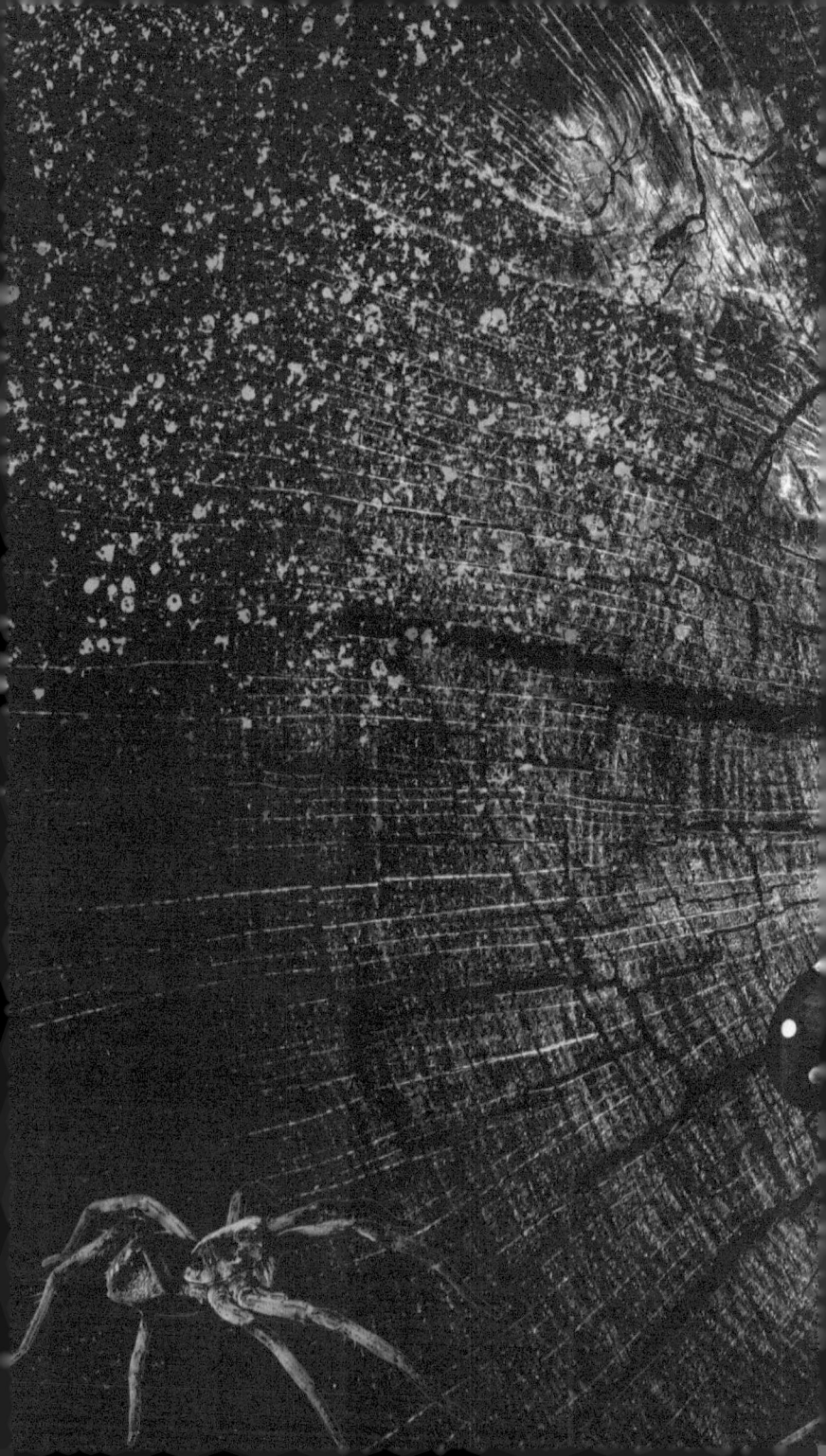

CHAPTER 14
Brooklyn

I want this man on me right now, devouring every inch of me. Just through this short time, I have learned that control is not for me. I would rather submit myself to him and all the things he can do to me, so I do.

"Yes," I get out as he begins to put his mouth back on my nipple. I grab his hand and begin to lower his fingers to my clit. He slowly begins to move them back and forth, quickening his pace with every second. He slid two fingers in me and hit my G-spot. Before I know it, he is bringing me to the edge.

I decide to switch things up a little bit and take the blood from both of the cuts made and mix it together to place on his tongue. His dick begins to harden again, showing that he is ready for round two. I don't give into him fucking me just yet. Instead, I grab some more blood and begin to stroke him up and down with my blood-coated hand.

Something about how we are set up right now has my body growing with the need for him to be inside of me, but I know we aren't at that point just yet. With both of our bodies naked, I decide we need to have one more round of this game before we can give in to what we came here tonight to do.

"This is the last time I am going to chase you. I want you to make it worth it this time. I will give you a hint and tell you at the next turn, you need to make a left, but after that, you are on your own. I will give you two minutes, and then I'll come after you," I begin to say before he starts to run again.

I keep to my word and give him two minutes to run. When that time is up, I make my way through the maze, where I take the next left turn. I decided to give him a little hint because I want him to feel like he actually has a chance this time when I know he doesn't.

I want to feel him under my body where I can edge him and make him experience everything that he wants to. I will also get what I want. I have some commands in mind that will help him know all the things that my body likes, but first I want to see what he is able to do.

I begin to think about how thankful I am for this experience because once it's over, we don't necessarily have to speak about it again. Having this once a year helps with a release that I know I have been needing for months without needing to make a commitment to someone.

CHAPTER 15
Brent

I am shocked that she wants to do one more round of this game between us, mainly because we are both naked this time. All I know is I am going to listen to what she says and carry out her demands. When she gave me the direction I needed to go, I was shocked. I thought she wanted me to suffer and not have a chance, but I learned that it was definitely not her.

Navigating through this cornfield has been pretty easy. The more I navigate it, the more I can tell the changes in the maze that hint at what way to go next. There are small markers within that you wouldn't be able to catch unless you have an eye for that thing. Luckily, I do.

I keep running, but before I know it, I am being tackled to the ground by the naked woman in the black and red mask. I don't know how to feel about it. The fact that she has the strength to knock me down has me shocked as hell, but I'm also happy that I can feel her on top of me. If I would have made it a few more steps, then I would have made it out of the maze, and she would not have caught me. She is definitely a fast little thing.

Part of me feels worried about what will happen next, but part of me is excited because I get to spend some more time with her. I want to feel her pretty pussy wrapped around my cock, but I am going to go at her pace from here on out.

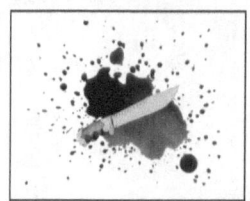

Brooklyn

Luckily, I was able to catch up to him right before the maze ended. I am grateful I ran track back in high school because it has given me a leg up in any type of chase game. If I wasn't as fast and he had gotten out before I had him inside of me, then I don't know how I would have felt.

I still have plans for the two of us, so he better be ready for what is to come next.

When I land on him, I can see how shocked he is that someone like me could tackle him to the ground.

"You thought you were getting out of here," I say with a sinister laugh. "This is what I have been waiting for all night."

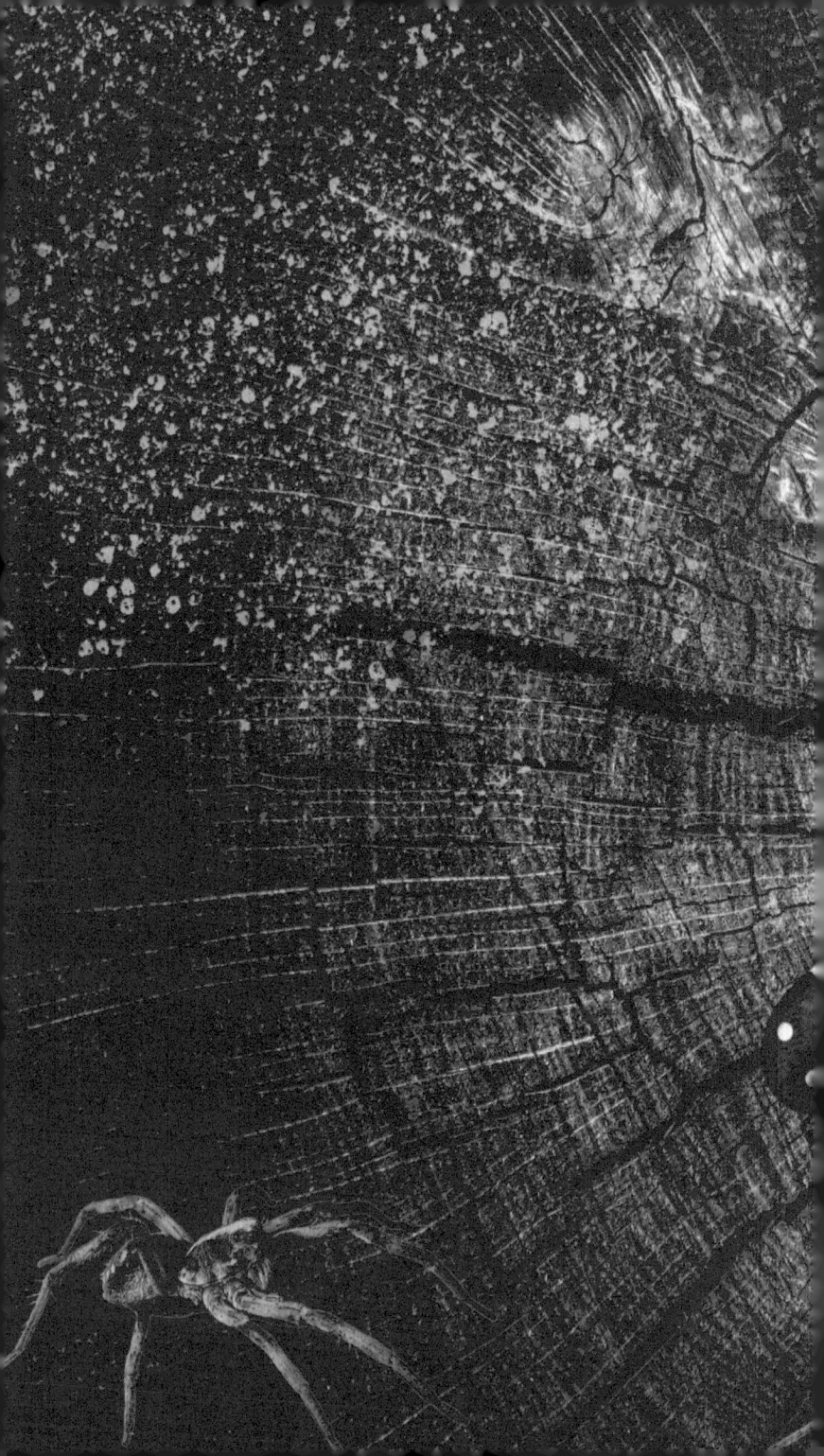

CHAPTER 16
Brooklyn

When Kelly told me before about the guy getting her off with the corn, it made me put that at the top of my bucket list. So, of course, this will happen tonight as long as Brent knows what he is doing.

After a few seconds, I move Brent to where I am straddling him. I contemplate for a moment if I should take my mask off so he can see my face. This is something that traditionally hasn't been done, but I feel that if we are going to be truly intimate, then he can see who I am.

I slowly lift my mask off my face when Brent begins to smile and says, "damn, babe, you really are beautiful" At this moment, any insecurities I had about myself disappeared from my mind. It is very rare to have a man as stunning as him say this about me, so I am going to soak up every second of this moment.

I can't tell by his reaction if he knows who I am or not, but the way he is looking at me shows that it doesn't matter right now. He slowly brings his hand up to my face and caresses the right side of my cheek. His touch is warm, but it is everything that I need right now.

I know this event is supposed to allow us to move fast while playing, but I think taking things slow is needed sometimes. I place my hand over his while leaning in to plant a soft kiss on his lips.

The air is thick with the sexual tension between the two of us. We quicken the pace of our kiss, and before I know it, I am climbing on top of him. The fact that we are both naked right now has me knowing what will come next. I just have to figure out what I want to happen first.

CHAPTER 17

Brent

Seeing how beautiful Brooklyn is has made me want to take her right now, but I let her take the lead. When she plants herself on top of me, my dick hardens with the need to the point that I know she can feel it.

I slowly lower my fingers down her breasts to her clit and begin to rub her in circles. "Fuck Brent," she moans out. I can feel her getting wetter by the second. I begin to enter two of my fingers inside her wet pussy and slowly pick up the pace. She begins to squirm in my lap as she reaches toward my dick to stroke me up and down.

Her hand fits around my length perfectly. The way her hand moves makes me need more. I decided why not change things up a little since we are in the middle of a cornfield maze.

I reach behind me and grab a piece of corn from one of the corn stalks. Her eyes grow big when she blurts out, "What the hell do you think you are going to do with that?" I shoot her a wink and begin to lower the corn to her clit where I slowly move it back and forth. She slowly starts to tense up with the movement.

"Baby, relax. I promise I won't do anything that is going to hurt you," I say.

She nods while saying, "I know you won't, but can you please stop teasing me and put it inside of me. I have been told the feeling is amazing."

Say less, I think to myself. I move her off of me and gently push her back onto the ground so that her bare pussy is completely exposed to me. She wants to experience this, but I need to get a taste of what I am working with first.

I slowly move to bury my face in between her legs and lap at her wet pussy, as a gasp comes out of her mouth. "Relax," I say as I continue to taste how sweet she is. I take the corn cob and slowly insert it inside of her, until she is fully filled.

I continue to move the corn in and out of her, picking up the speed with each thrust. She continues to let out low moans of pleasure, so I decide to gently nip at her clit with my teeth, causing her moans to get louder.

"That's it, baby girl. Don't hide your pleasure. I wish you could see how you look right now." I begin to see her body shutter, knowing she just had her first orgasm. I pull the corn out of her, and she immediately comes towards me and kisses me deeply.

CHAPTER 18
Brooklyn

Damn, the feel of Brent's tongue on my pussy, and the corn inside of me quickly set me over the edge. That had to be one of the best orgasms I have had in a long time. I know I want to feel him inside of me so I can see what he's capable of.

I climb back into his lap and slowly lower myself onto his dick. "Fuck," he groans, causing me to laugh.

"I didn't say I was going to give you a warning before I sat down on you. Just sit back and enjoy what I can do to you." I can see the smirk that comes across his face. I should've known that he wouldn't complain about where this was going.

I begin to pick up my speed as I bounce up and down on his dick, causing his grunts and moans to increase. I can sense that he's getting closer to his release, so I instantly stop moving, causing his dick to slowly twitch inside of me.

"You're such a tease," he says as he goes to grab my hips. I swat his hands away from me and grab my knife that I have from when I was running earlier. Shockingly, this doesn't phase him at all. Maybe he has something for blood like I do.

I take the knife and run it from the top of his chest down to his pelvis bone, being sure to not dig too deep but just enough to draw some blood. I love the sight before me. I run my finger along the trail that I created and place it into my mouth so I can get another taste of him.

"Mmh, you taste so good," I let out as I began to move up and down on his dick again.

"Well damn, I think you should let me get another taste of you as well," he says with hunger in his eyes.

I slow down as I ride him to make a small cut along the side of my arm to draw a little bit of blood to allow him to get another taste. He licks his lips and says, "You taste so nice and good, I could get used to this."

"You sound like a vampire," I let out a laugh, causing him to laugh as well.

Him being into blood and having the same kink

as me is turning me on even more. I pick up my pace with the need to cum.

Before I know it, we are both chasing our releases.

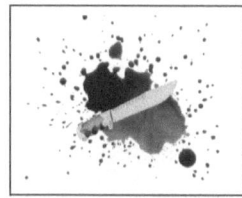

After everything that we did, we are just lying here on the ground of the cornfield maze. Luckily, it is just the two of us, so we are able to relax together after catching our release.

I know The Chase is about having the cat-and-mouse game as long as you can, but I am happy with the way things are currently going. There is just something about Brent that draws me in and makes me want to surrender to anything he wants to do to me and what he needs.

Part of me doesn't want the night to end because I don't want this to be the last night I have with him.

"Brent," I say with a shaky voice.

He turns on his side and says, "Yes, beautiful."

Something about him calling me beautiful again brings joy to my heart.

"Do you think you would want to meet up again

after this? I know this is supposed to be a one-night experience, but there is just something about you that I would love to continue to get to know."

His eyes seem to brighten with the question. "I would love that," he says with an exciting tone to his voice.

CHAPTER 19

Brent

I am shocked to hear that Brooklyn wants to meet up again after this night is over. That is something that is not traditional for events such as this one. Usually, what happens out here stays out here, and then people go about their lives.

Something about her is different, though, and I am glad that she has decided to want to spend more time with me.

I quickly get out of my thoughts and lean in to plant another kiss on Brooklyn's lips.

"You ready to get dressed and get out of here?" I ask.

"Yeah, let's go," she lets out, causing us to go search for our clothes scattered throughout the maze.

After we find our clothes and get dressed, we walk

to the exit of the maze in silence. I think we are both contemplating what we want to do and say next.

When we got to the area where The Chase started, we grabbed our phones from the secure area where we had to place them.

I break the silence and ask, "Can I see your phone so I can put my number into it?"

She hands over her phone. I put my number in then send myself a text message so I have her number as well.

About an hour later, I get home and wash away the night's festivities from my body. I want to send her a text message, but I don't want to seem too desperate, so I end up putting my phone on the charger and head to sleep for the night.

I wake to the doorbell ringing. *Who the hell could be here right now disturbing my peace this early in the morning*, I think to myself.

I look down at my phone and notice it's already 2:00 in the afternoon, and I have a ton of text messages in our group chat from the guys, making sure I am still alive and good.

Alex: Hey, you up?

Nate: Dude, you better be up; it is already in the afternoon.

Michael: I feel like he must still be sleeping.

Alex: He better not be.

Michael: Maybe we should go to his house and see what he is doing.

Nate: What if he has some girl there, then what?

Alex: I really doubt he does. He went home by himself last night.

Michael: Alright, I will meet you guys there in 10 minutes.

Whoops. I didn't mean to sleep that long. They make it seem like I am dead.

I climb out of bed and head to the door; before I can fully get it open, Alex, Nate, and Michael are all barging in.

"What the hell happened to you? We have been trying to get in contact with you all morning, but you haven't been answering," Alex says with frustration in his voice.

"I'm sorry; I had a long night and didn't realize I didn't set an alarm to get up this morning."

"What do you mean a long night? You told us you went home and were lying down," Nate said.

My eyes start to wander in a different direction. "About that...," I say with hesitation in my tone. The guys have a mixture of confusion and frustration on their faces as if they don't know where this will go..

"Take a seat, and we can talk about what actually happened last night," I say, a little nervous.

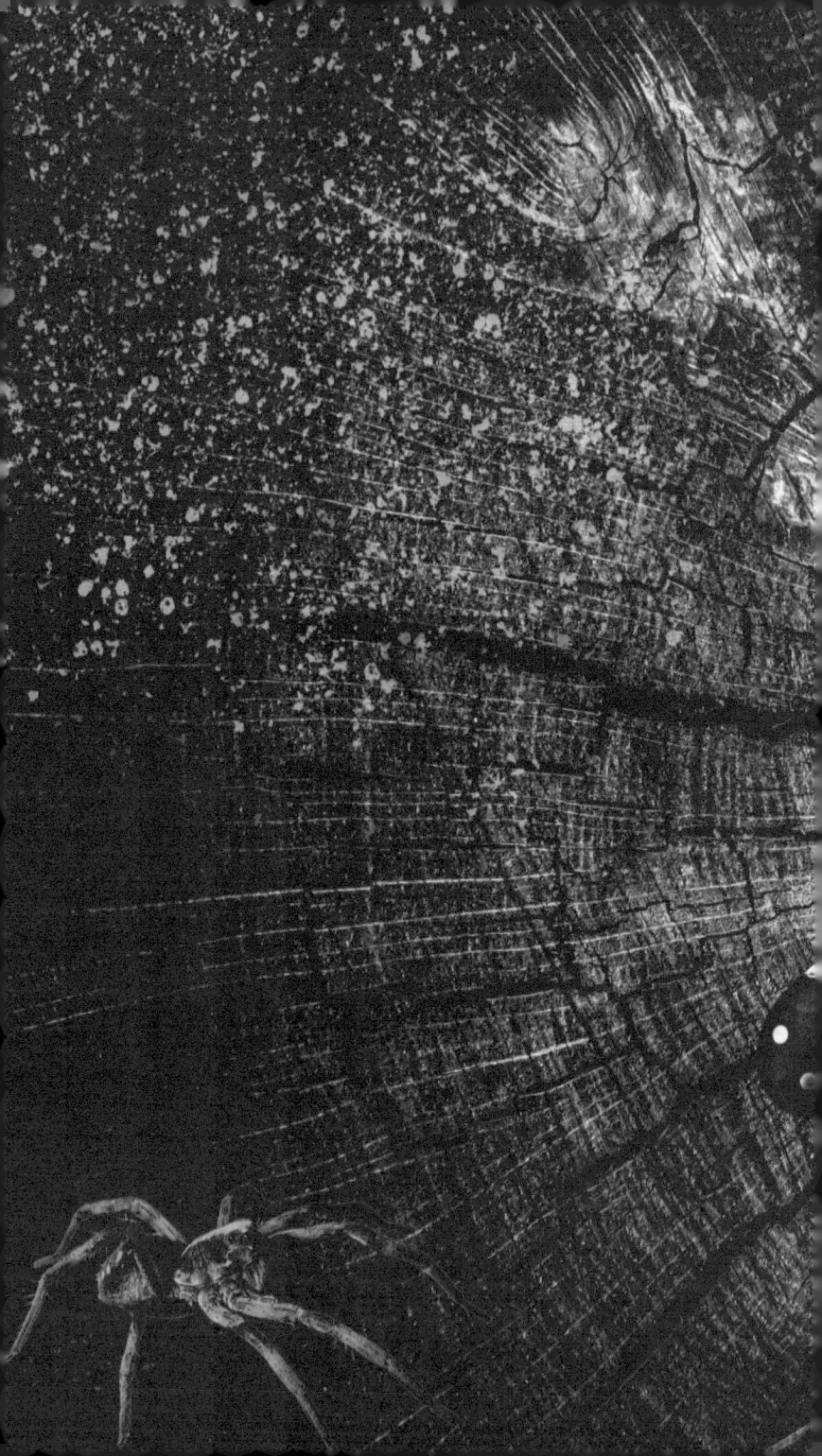

CHAPTER 20

Brooklyn

While at lunch this morning with Kelly and Janet, I kept checking my phone, thinking I would have a text message from Brent, but I thought wrong. I guess I should have known it was too good to be true.

I wonder if all of the positive words he said about me last night were just for show or if he truly meant them. If he had meant them, I would have thought he would have reached out by now.

"Earth to Brooklyn. Are you there? I asked you a question," Kelly says, pulling me out of the trance I put myself into.

"I'm sorry, I'm here. What did you say?"

"Janet asked you how the rest of your night went when we split up."

Shit, I don't even know where to begin with

telling them about my experience. There was so much that happened. I don't know if I should tell them that I exchanged numbers with Brent or not.

"Well, the night was great. We were able to explore each other's blood play kink, which, shockingly, he was into more than I thought he would. He even decided to use a piece of corn on me, which I completely loved. I feel like I had some type of connection with him that I haven't had with anyone in a long time, so we ended up exchanging numbers. But unfortunately, I haven't heard from him, so maybe he has second thoughts about what happened," I say with a defeated look on my face.

Kelly and Janet both look at each other to determine who is going to say something, causing Janet to speak up first.

"Babe, I'm happy that you had fun, but don't think negatively. Maybe he's still asleep, or he is out with his friends. I wouldn't overthink things. You are such a catch, so I doubt he will be able to resist you if you meet up again."

"You could also send him a text, too. Maybe he is waiting to see if you have any regrets," Kelly blurts out.

I think about what they both say for a moment and decide what is the best route for me to take. I ultimately pull my phone out and send a simple text message.

> Me: Thank you for the good night last night.

"Sent, we will see what happens next."

Hopefully.

CHAPTER 21

Brent

Right before I told the guys about how my night went, my phone pinged with a text message.

> Brooklyn: Thank you for the good night last night.

Shoot, I wanted to be the one to send the text message first. Now I feel like an ass because she probably thought I was ghosting her after the night we had.

"Brent, you good? You look like you have seen a ghost," Michael says.

"I'm alright. I just might have fucked up a little bit."

I go on to tell the guys about the night that I had with Brooklyn, and they seem intrigued by what I am saying. Shockingly, they aren't mad that I lied about going home.

"Text her back and ask her to meet up," Michael suggests, so I send off a text.

> Me: Hey, I enjoyed last night too. Do you want to meet up tonight for dinner around 6pm at Vino's and talk more?

I instantly get a text back from her.

> Brooklyn: I would love that, I will see you then.

I can't stop a smile from filling my face.

A few hours go by before it's finally time for me to get ready for tonight's date. I can't wait to meet up with Brooklyn, get to know more about her, and see how things could go from here. It's crazy to think something that should have only been one night is taking a turn to what I hope is for the better.

I end up throwing on a pair of black jeans with a

red polo shirt. I slick back my hair, and I am ready to go.

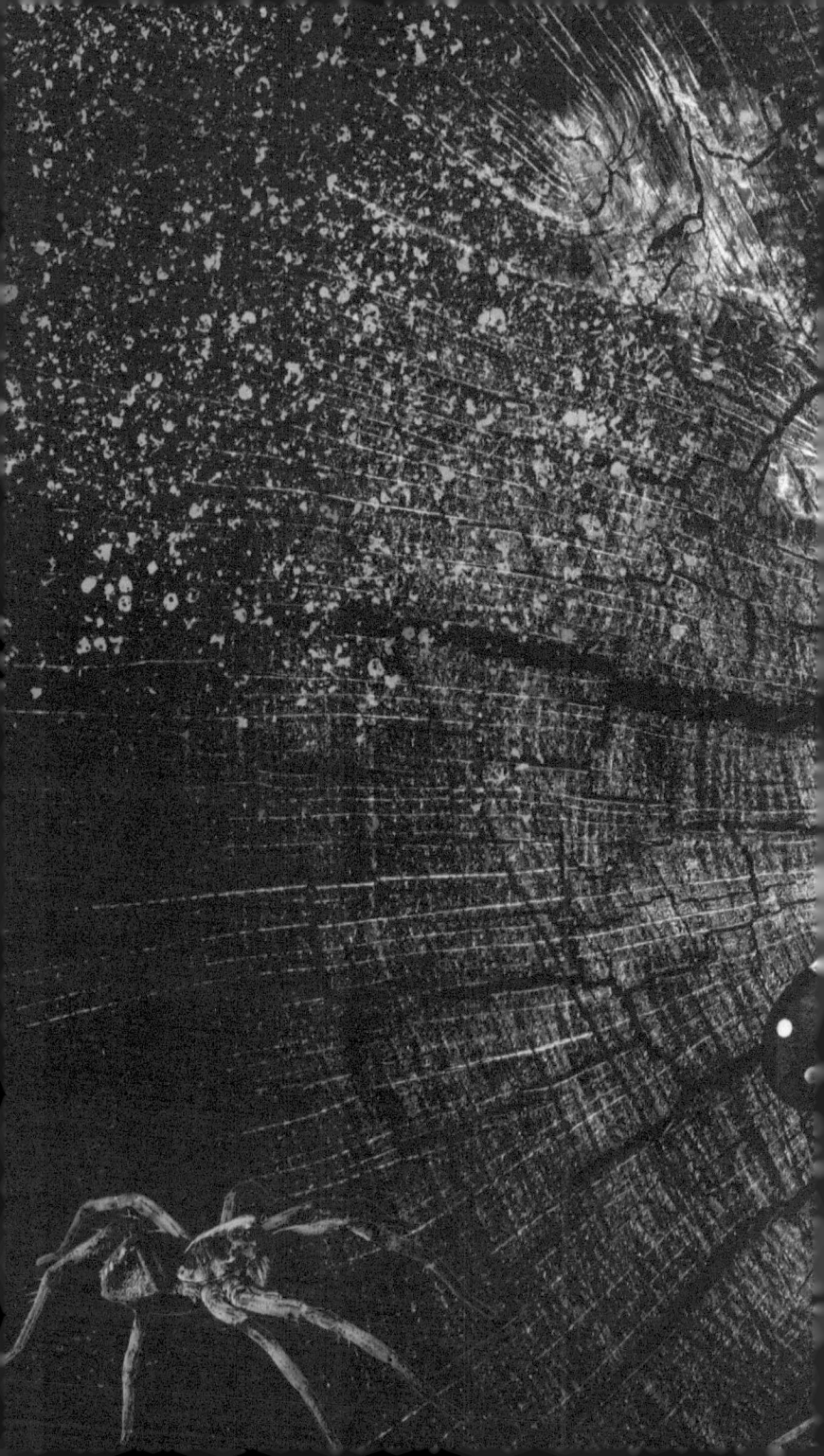

CHAPTER 22
Brooklyn

When the girls and I finished brunch, I received a text back from Brent asking me to meet tonight for dinner. I squeal with excitement, and the girls think I'm crazy until I show them the message.

"We have to find you the perfect outfit for tonight," Kelly says as she throws some cash on the table to pay for our tab.

We quickly get up and head back to my apartment to figure out what I am going to wear, even though the date is still a few hours away. Ultimately, I settle on a red knee-length dress and a pair of black heels. Something simple, but sexy.

While I wait for the time of my date to come around, I decide to pull out my e-reader and continue with one of my dark romances. Reading these types of books gave me ideas of what to do last night during The Chase.

I often find myself getting lost in the words of the books I read because I tune out the rest of the world around me. I love seeing how enemies become lovers or how women get stalked through the night by the handsome man who will do anything to make sure she is safe.

Not everyone has the same taste in books that I do, but I find that to be okay. As long as we don't kink shame each other, then I am completely fine.

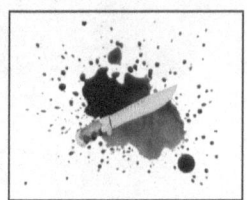

After getting lost in my book for a few hours, my alarm rings, notifying me that it's time for me to get ready for my date.

I slip on the red dress and black heels and put some curls in my hair. I opt for minimal makeup tonight.. He has seen me without makeup on and in the most vulnerable way and I want to show him that side of me again.

I take one last look at myself in the mirror and determine I'm good to go for the night. I hop into my SUV and head to Vino's. I've heard of this place before, but I have never actually been, so I am excited to try the food.

When I arrive at the restaurant, I see Brent standing by the front door, looking nervous as he waits for me. It is kind of cute to see a guy nervous when I am just an average girl.

I check myself one last time in the mirror of my car and decide I look as best as I am going to be. I hop out of the car and head towards where Brent is waiting for me.

CHAPTER 23

Brent

D amn. As I see Brooklyn walking my way, that is all I can think of. She is in a beautiful red dress that hugs her curves perfectly. She must have something for the color red since that is the color she was wearing last night too. I think it is kind of cute that we are also matching right now.

I don't know if I should shake her hand or lean in for a hug, so I go for the latter decision and give her a hug. Shock appears on her face, and I feel like I might have done something wrong already.

"I'm sorry for hugging you if that made you uncomfortable," I say, but she interrupts me by placing a kiss on my lips.

"You didn't make me uncomfortable at all. Let's head inside."

I feel like my body is in a sense of shock at the

fact that she just kissed me. If I had known that was the route she was going to go, then I definitely would have done that instead of going in for an awkward hug.

I get out of my thoughts, open the door for her, and tell the host about the reservation I have for two. The host escorts us to a booth in the back corner of the restaurant, which is nice because we don't have to worry about others overhearing our conversation.

"Thank you for joining me tonight on such short notice. I am glad I was able to see you again because I enjoyed your free spirit last night. It was such a good vibe."

She let out a laugh, and confusion struck my face about what was so funny.

"Who says it's a good vibe anymore," she says as she continues to laugh. Maybe I am just a little old school because that is something that I often say.

"Oh, you know, just little old me," I say with a smile on my face. I feel like she'll be able to match my energy, and we will have a good time together.

The server comes over, and we order a bottle of red wine to split, and each get a dish of pasta for dinner.

We begin to chat and get to know each other, and the conversation flows easily.

"Tell me a little about what you do for a living," I question with curiosity in my tone.

"I am a Licensed Clinical Social Worker who provides therapy to children and families after a traumatic event. I often engage in short-term symptom-based therapy that helps these individuals be able to return to their baseline by providing coping strategies. It is a hard job sometimes, but it is rewarding to see the decrease in symptoms they experience after the short-term therapy. I also run a daycare center as well, which has been nice because I can use my social work skills when interacting with the children in the center. What about you?"

I am in complete awe of this woman. I knew there was something about her that I was going to enjoy, and seeing how she helps children and families just makes me happy, and my heart fills with joy. I go back and forth on whether I should be honest about what I do for a living or not. Often, when people hear what I do, they just want to use me for my money, but something feels different about her.

"Your job definitely sounds rewarding. I, on the other hand, am a little boring. I am a business owner of a gaming company. We create a wide range of games that you can find in stores all around the world," I say while looking to see how she is going to respond.

Luckily, she doesn't have a change in facial expressions to that. Instead, she says, "I would love to learn more about the games you create one day. Maybe we could play one together, and you could show me the ropes of everything."

I feel like I am at a loss for words. I have never met someone who wanted to learn more about my world before and what I do, so seeing that she is interested makes me so happy.

"I would love to show you what I do," I say as the waitress comes over with our food.

We continue to make small talk in between bites, getting to know each other better and on a deeper level.

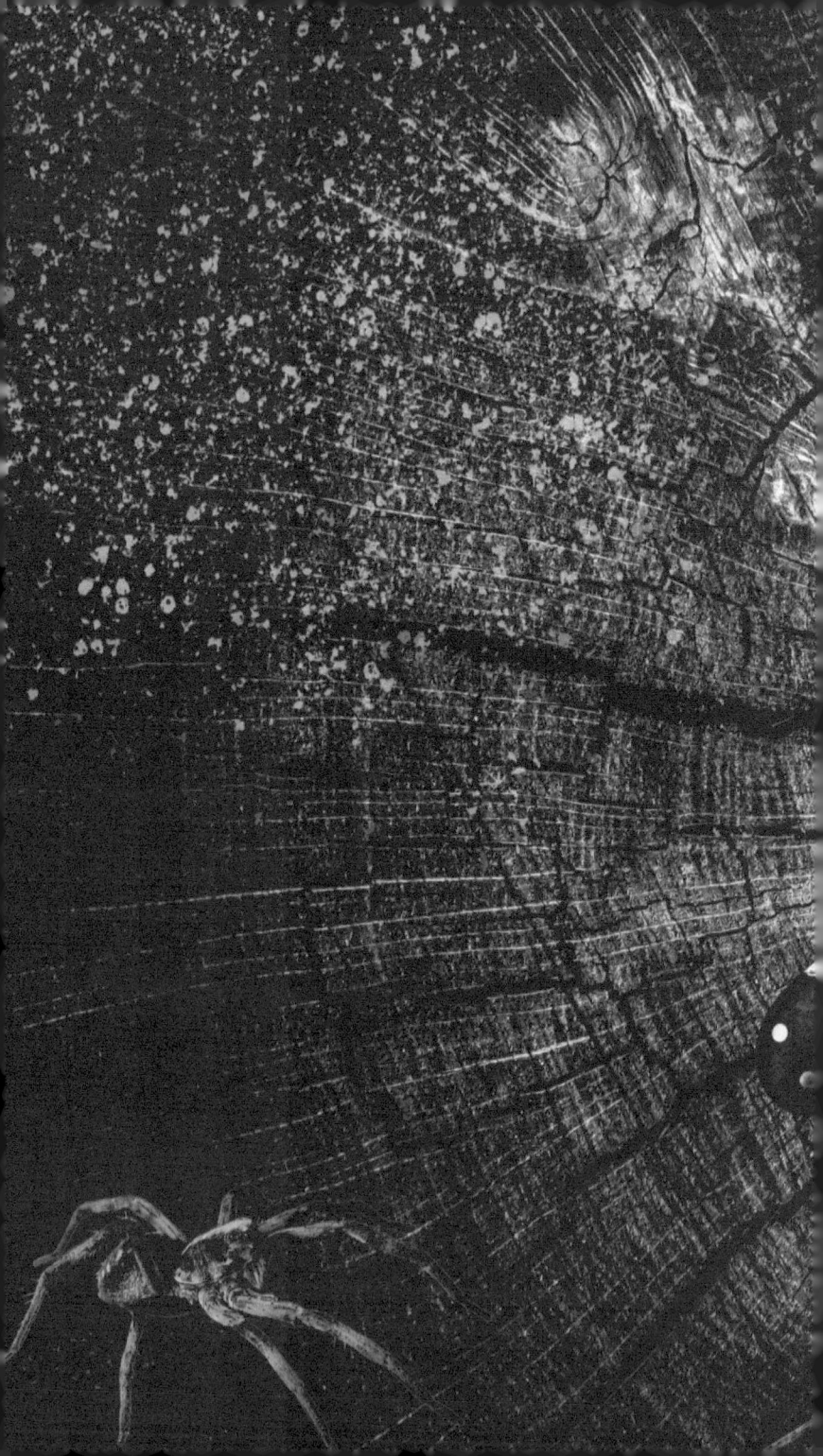

CHAPTER 24

Brooklyn

I love getting to know Brent more. He is a completely open book and has a good sense of humor. There is just something about him that just makes us click.

Before I know it, the waitress is coming with our checks, which means the night is unfortunately coming to an end.

"Do you want to come back to my place for a little while and maybe watch a movie? I've enjoyed spending time with you, and I don't want this night to end just yet," I admit to him.

He agrees, so I text him my address, and we head that way.

When we get to my house, I head to my room and throw on a comfortable pair of pajamas.

I pop some popcorn, and we decide to open another bottle of wine to drink during the movie. Both of us love watching scary movies, so we opt for one of the slasher films that has a lot of gore and blood. *Only we would enjoy something like this.*

We snuggle up on the couch and hit play on the movie. The movie feels like it is over to soon.

"It's been a good night so far," I turn to Brent and say.

"I agree. Thank you for being willing to have dinner with me and take the chance to get to know me better. I'm going to head out, but I will definitely keep in touch with you," he says.

I really don't want this night to end, but it is probably for the best for now. "Get home safe, and let me know when you make it," I plant a kiss on his lips.

"I will," he says as he walks out the front door.

About ten minutes later, I get a text from him.

Brent: I made it home safely. We should definitely do this again sometime.

Me: I agree. I know we will have a blast any other time we hang out. You definitely have to show me how to play the games you help create.

Brent: I definitely will. Get some sleep, goodnight, beautiful.

Me: Goodnight *heart emoji*

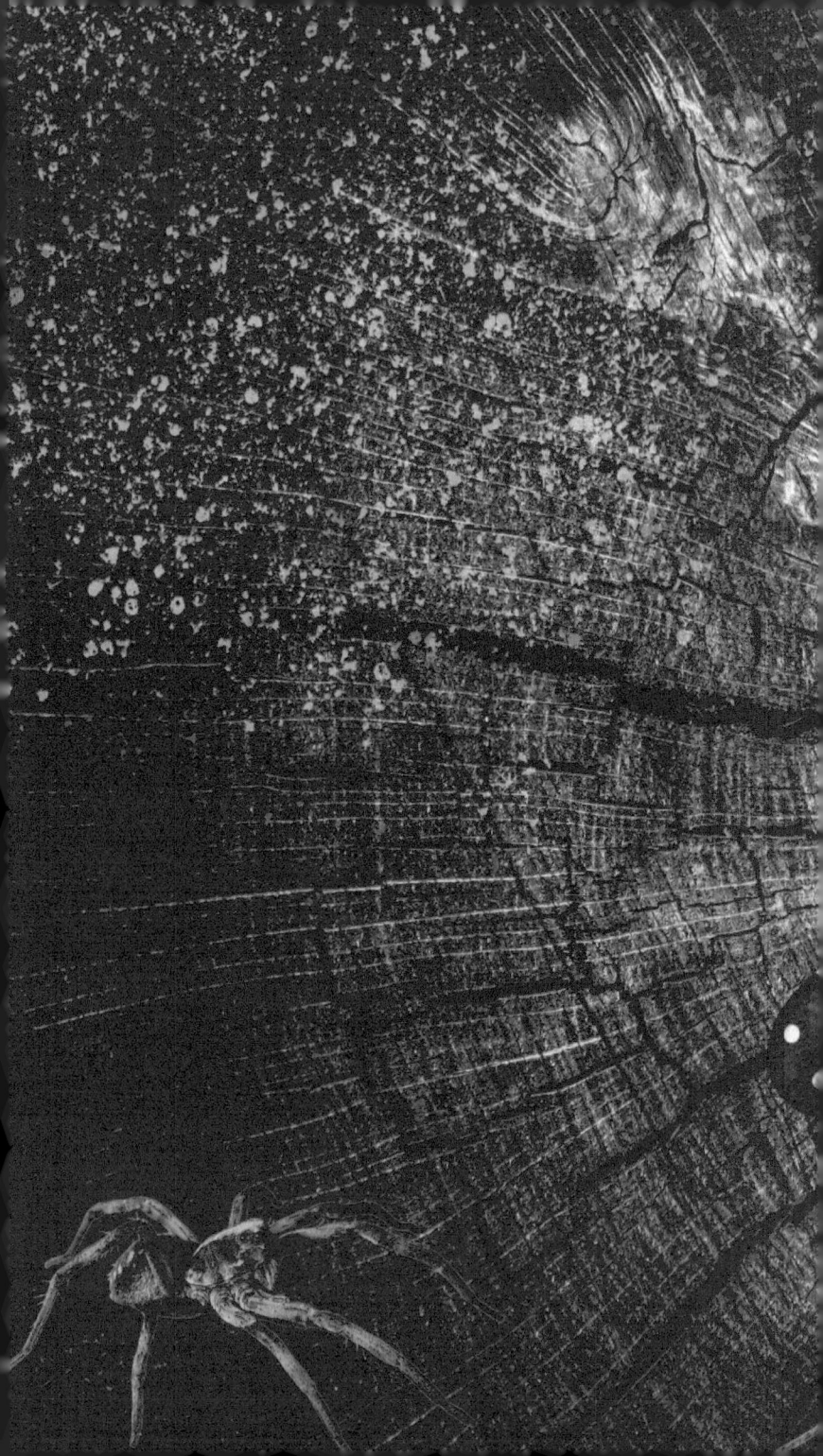

CHAPTER 25

Brooklyn

Three months have passed since I met Brent, and I love every second of our relationship. We have gotten to know each other on such a deeper level. Recently, I found out he is a billionaire from the gaming company that he owns, but that hasn't changed anything between us. I have never been one to be with someone because of their money.

A month into hanging out, we sat down and talked about wanting to test things out between us, so he asked me to be his girlfriend and since then everything has been going great. I was able to officially meet his best friends, and he was able to meet mine.

Brent and I agreed that we wanted to take things slow between the two of us starting off, even though we started things off in the most unconventional way. I feel like I am ready to take things to the next level when he is prepared to do so because there is just something about him that makes me know that he is the one for me.

Ever since the maze, we have talked about our future goals in life, and most of our goals have aligned. We have built such a deep connection with one another. Our career path was one of the biggest things we discussed. I want to continue my therapist job, which he is completely supportive of.

Tonight, we have all decided to go to one of the winter festivals to look at the lights and decorations for Christmas. It's crazy to think about how we are already in the Christmas season.

As Brent is driving with me in the passenger seat, I hold his hand, and we sing along to Christmas songs until we arrive at the festival site.

The lights are stunning as we get out of the van. We each head to the big tree in the front of the building to take pictures together. Little did I know tonight would be the night when everything would change.

When Brent and I get ready for a picture together, he gets down on one knee, which instantly makes me tear up.

"Brooklyn, when we met, I knew it was supposed to be a one-night thing, but at that moment, I knew I could never let you go. The past few months have been amazing with you. I know I don't want to do life without you moving forward..." he begins to say as he pulls out a ring. "Will you make me the happiest man on this Earth and be my wife?"

The floodgates of tears immediately open up as I choke out the words, "Of course I will." I look over and see Kelly and Janet balling their eyes out with excitement beside Alex, Michael, and Nate.

I genuinely don't know what I would do without Brent, but what I do know is I can't wait to spend the rest of my life with him.

Epilogue: Brent

This past year has been both wonderful and challenging. Wedding planning has been a pain in the ass. Who would have known there are so many different shades of blues and yellows to pick from.

Luckily, Brooklyn and her friends have been able to do the bulk of the wedding planning because I want her to have her dream wedding.

As I am getting ready today alongside my friends, I am overwhelmed with joy that the next chapter of my life is about to start as a married man. If you had asked me two years ago where I would be today, I definitely wouldn't say in this predicament. I was always so focused on work to live up to the expectations of my father when he passed away, that I didn't make time for women in my life. Ultimately, I am glad that this decision was made.

When the ceremony starts, I head to the altar, waiting for my beautiful bride to walk down it. She is dressed in a long white gown with lace on the front and a veil that hangs to the ground attached to her hair.

Brooklyn is absolutely stunning.

As she approaches the altar, a small teardrop falls down my face. I told myself I wouldn't cry, but being here right now, those thoughts went entirely out the window. She is fantastic and is about to be mine for eternity.

Our wedding ceremony goes fast, and before I know it, we are being pronounced Mr. and Mrs. West. This is absolutely one of the best days of my life.

I can't believe one night of being stalked in a cornfield is now turning into a lifetime of joy and memories.

Acknowledgments

I am thankful for my husband Markus for telling me to keep writing and to try something new.

Thank you to my alpha and beta readers for providing me with feedback on my book, and helping me ensure it sounds good before I released it.

I would like to thank my street team for helping to promote this book, and get it discovered by those in the world!

Paula, I am thankful for the character art you created for the cover of this book. You brought my vision to light and I absolutely love it! Thank you for all you do and continue to do!

Deann Soleil ☼

About the Author

Deann Soleil is a self-published author based in Virginia who focuses on writing forbidden romances. When not writing, she is a full-time social worker who works with victims of community violence to help them overcome their traumatic experiences.

If you're looking for short, fast-paced books, then look no further.

Also by Deann Soleil

Consumed

Chasing the Forbidden Desire

A Wild Run Anthology (The Chase)

Monsters, Masks & Mayhem Anthology (The Graveyard)

Tangled Up With Santa (Coming in December of 2025)